P9-DYE-035

This book belongs to:
Pinkster

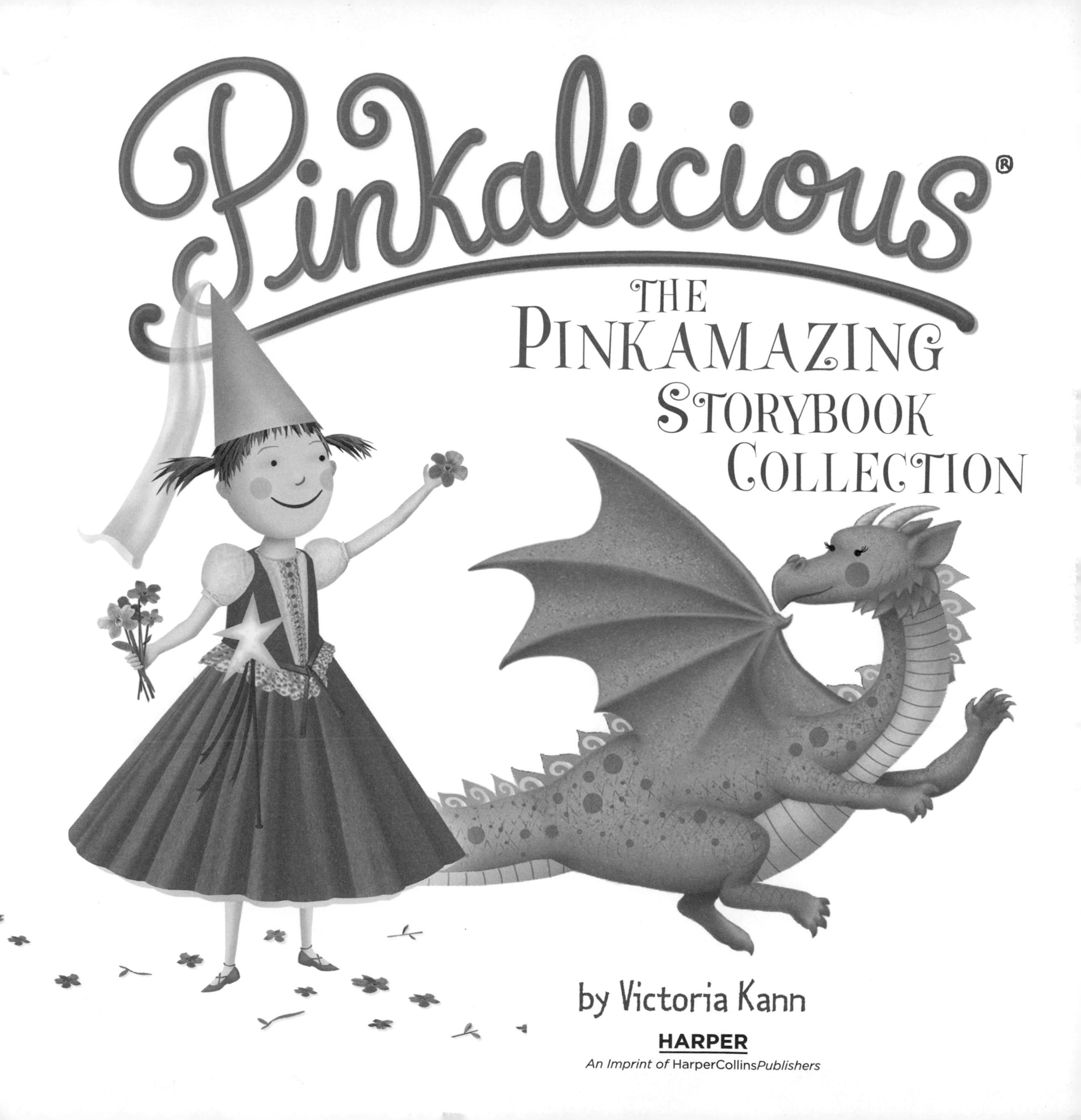
Pinkalicious®
THE
PINKAMAZING
STORYBOOK
COLLECTION
by Victoria Kann
HARPER
An Imprint of HarperCollinsPublishers

Table of Contents

Pinkalicious
The Pinkerrific Playdate
by
Victoria Kann

For Eileen and Esa!

xox,

V.K.

by Victoria Kann

I have a new friend.

Her name is Rose.

The wonderful thing about Rose

is that we have a great time

playing together.

Last week,
I didn't even know Rose's name.
All I knew about Rose
was that she was new at our school.

On Thursday, Alison said,

“Let’s jump with both ropes.”

“We can’t,” I said.

“We need three people for that.”

“What about the new girl,
Rose?” Alison asked.
“What a beautiful name,” I said.
“Let’s ask her to play, too.”

Rose could really jump!

Rose sat with us at lunch.

I shared my pink cupcakes.

Alison shared her beet salad.

Rose shared her strawberry smoothie.

Sharing is wonderful.

So is Rose!

Today, Alison has soccer.

Rose is coming over for a playdate

for the first time ever.

I can hardly wait!

"What are you going to do together?" asked Peter.

"It's all planned," I said.

"Is it time yet?" I asked Mommy.

"I'm so excited.

I can't wait!"

"Rose will have a wonderful time.

You've planned so much to do!"

said Mommy.

dominoes
cartwheels
tree house
jump rope
draw
make friendship bracelets
hula hoops
play princess
bake cookies
Yummy!
tea party with Dolly and Rabbit
checkers

“This will be fun!” said Peter.

“You’re not exactly invited,” I said.

“Don’t forget to include Peter, Pinkalicious,” said Mommy.

Just then, the doorbell rang.

It was Rose!

"Come on, Rose," I said.

"Let's make friendship bracelets!"

"I like the colors you picked,"

said Rose.

"I like your colors, too," I told her.

“Look at me!

I’m playing, too,” said Peter.

"It's time to bake cookies," I said.

"Pink sprinkles go on top!"

“Yummy!” said Rose.

“Fumfy,” said Peter.

His mouth was full.

“Now it’s hula hoop time!” I said.

Rose and I ran outside.

Peter came, too.

“I can hula two hoops!” said Rose.

“Me, too!” I said.

We talked about our favorite books.

We talked about our best birthdays so far.

We talked about our teacher

and the ice-skating rink.

We talked a lot.

Then we giggled about
our little brothers.
Rose has one, too!
I forgot all about my list
of things to do.

"Time to go," Rose's mom said.

"What?" Rose said.

"We didn't get to play dress-up,

or do the obstacle course,

or do the limbo," I wailed.

"I love to do the limbo,"

Rose said.

"Can we do that next time?"

She smiled at me.

I smiled back.

Peter smiled, too.

"This was the best playdate ever!"

he said.

"I think so, too, Peter!"

Rose said.

I smiled.

"Me, too!"

Pinkalicious

and the Pink Hat Parade

PINK IS PERFECT

by
Victoria Kann

For the very creative and stylish
Marcella, Ainsleigh, Russell,
Wendy, and Chris
—V.K.

Pinkalicious®

and the Pink Hat Parade

by Victoria Kann

I was eating my breakfast of pink pancakes with peaches when Mommy walked into the kitchen.

1 QUART
1 Qt.
1½ Pt.
1 Pt.
½ Pt.

"Guess what, you two," she said to me and Peter. "It's almost time for your favorite day ever!"

"My birthday?" said Peter.

"National Pink Day?" I said.

"No," said Mommy. "The Spring Fling! The fun starts tomorrow."

"Yes!" we exclaimed. The Spring Fling was our neighborhood party.

The best part was the Hat Parade and contest. Every year I make a pinkatastic hat and dress up in pink to show it off.

cup milk

"This year, my hat is going to win the grand prize!" said Peter.

Peter gobbled up the rest of his breakfast and ran over to Mommy to whisper something in her ear. "Okay," she said. "But not too many."

In a flash, Peter grabbed something from the kitchen cabinet. It's a good thing I was paying attention, because I almost missed what he took with him: a bag of chocolate candy. I guess he needed something sweet to munch on as we worked. I helped myself to a piece of chocolate, too.

When I got back to my room, I grabbed my pink pen and got to work.

By that afternoon, my room was a huge mess. I carefully glued flowers and butterflies onto my hat. Then I made a sash that said "PINK IS PERFECT." It looked pinkatastic.

PINK IS PERFECT

I went over to Peter's room to see what he was doing.

"Peter is still working on his hat, Pinkalicious," said Mommy. "In fact, Daddy just went out to get him a few more bags of chocolate."

A few more bags? I knew Peter liked chocolate, but this was getting ridiculous!

That night at dinner, Peter came into the kitchen looking tired but with a huge smile on his face. "I finished my hat," he said proudly. "It's so sweet! I'm definitely going to win the contest tomorrow."

"That's what you think," I said, but Peter wasn't listening. He had a funny look on his face and I could tell he was imagining himself taking home the big prize.

The next morning, I put on my pinkest dress. Peter and I rushed through breakfast and grabbed our hatboxes.

We stepped out the door and into a roaring block party. Our neighborhood was transformed! Everything looked amazing in the bright sunlight.

"Let's hurry, Pinkalicious," said Peter, grabbing my hand. "The parade is going to start any minute!" We dodged past a boy with a balloon and swerved around the cotton candy machine. By the time we got to the spot where everyone was lining up, I was hot and thirsty.

It was finally time for the parade. I took my hat out of the box and put it on right away. The beautiful paper flowers and butterflies I had made sparkled in the sunlight. "Peter," I said. "Don't I look perfectly pink?"

Peter didn't answer. He was too busy trying to get his hat out of the box. "Help me, Pinkalicious!" he cried. "My hat is stuck!" I reached into the box to pull out the hat, when my hand felt something sticky.

"Peter!" I cried. "What is this stuff?"

The Pinkville

We tugged and tugged and tugged. When the hat finally came out of the box, I couldn't believe my eyes. My brother had made his hat ENTIRELY OUT OF CHOCOLATE.

"Come on, Pinkalicious!" Peter grinned, holding his creation proudly. He wiped away a bit of melted chocolate as he put the hat on his head. "Let's go!"

As we marched through the neighborhood, I walked proudly in my pinkatastic hat. It was the pinka-prettiest hat in the whole parade. Walking was a little tricky because I also had to make sure I didn't step in little pools of mud that lay in the path in front of me.

"That's weird," I said. "How come it's so muddy on such a hot day?"

That's when I realized what was going on. The little pools on the path weren't made out of mud. They were made out of chocolate.

"Oh, no!" I cried. Peter's hat was melting in the sun!

By the end of the parade, Peter was covered in chocolate. "You look like a chocolate monster," I said, giggling. Peter wasn't laughing, though. He looked like he was ready to cry.

"This was such a bad idea." He sniffled. "Let's go home."

We were about to turn around and leave when we heard the parade announcer clear his throat. "This year's winner for Best Hat is . . . Pinkalicious!" he said. The crowd cheered.

I smiled shyly as I went to get my trophy. I was happy to win, because I had worked hard on my hat. But I knew someone who had worked even harder.

Spring Fling
Hat Parade
PINK IS PERFECT

"Here, Peter," I said, giving him the trophy. "I think you deserve this."

"Really?" said Peter. "Why?"

"Your hat might not have turned out the way you wanted it to," I said, "but it was special. It was original. Most of all . . . it was *definitely* chocolicious!"

Pinkalicious

The Princess of Pink Slumber Party

by Victoria Kann

For Jennifer and Sydney
—V.K.

by Victoria Kann

I was having a slumber party.

It was not any old slumber party.

It was a Princess of Pink party!

My whole family got ready.
Mommy and Daddy dressed up
like a queen and a king.

“I’m the royal prince,” said Peter.

He grabbed a crown out of my hand.

“You’re more like a royal joker,”

I told him.

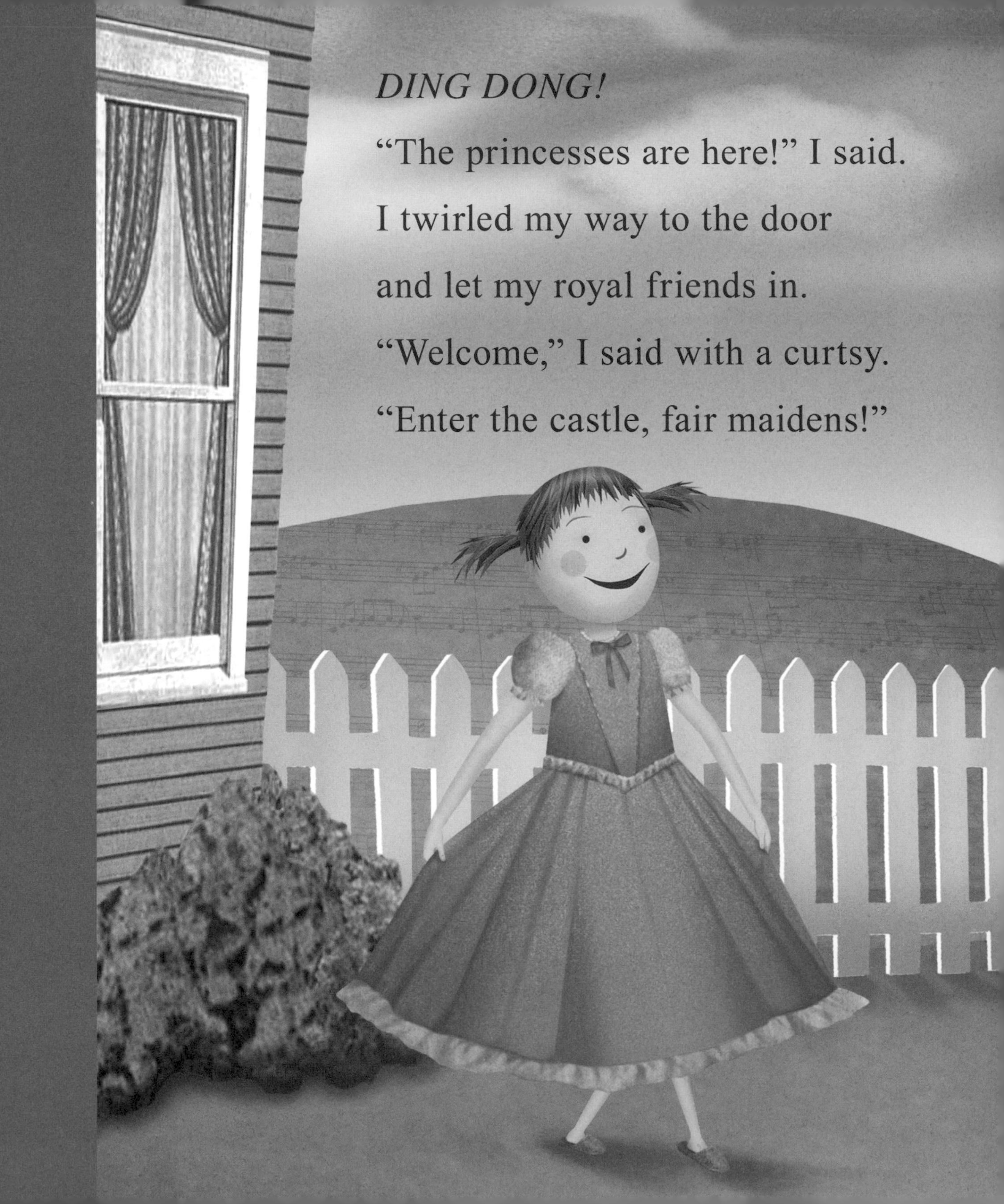

DING DONG!

"The princesses are here!" I said.

I twirled my way to the door

and let my royal friends in.

"Welcome," I said with a curtsy.

"Enter the castle, fair maidens!"

"How grand!" Molly said.

"I'm ready for the ball!" Rose said.

"Hello, Princess Alison," I said.

"Hi," Alison said quietly.

She held her bear tightly.

“Let’s play musical thrones!”
I started the music
and we danced around the chairs.
I didn’t even mind being
the last one left without a throne.

"Yay! I won!" said Molly.

"Your prize, Your Majesty," I said.

I handed Molly a pinkatastic wand.

"It's time to make tiaras!" I said.

"Ohhhh," Rose said.

"Look at the dazzling jewels!"

"My tiara is going to twinkle like a star," said Molly.

"Look at me," I said.

I put my tiara proudly on my head.

"I have the sparkliest tiara

in all the land!"

"Dinner is served!" said Mommy.

"We made a royal feast," said Daddy.

"Princess-and-the-Split-Pea Soup,

Chicken Nuggets à la King,

and Castle Cupcakes for dessert!"

Peter said, “If I was ruler,
we’d always eat dessert first!”
“Yum,” I said.
“That would be a very sweet kingdom!”

After dinner Peter climbed
to the top of a pile of pillows
and yelled, “I’m king of the castle!”

“It’s princess of the castle around here,” I said.

“Princesses rule!” Molly said.

Suddenly I heard a sniffle.
It came from Alison.
"What's wrong?" I asked her.
"I'm scared to sleep over,"
she whispered in my ear.
I gave Alison a hug.
"Sleeping away from home
can be kind of scary," I said.

“What would a real princess do
to make Alison feel better?” I asked.
“Protect her from villains!” Rose said.
“A princess faces her perils
with strength,” Molly said.
Alison still looked scared.

"I know!" I said.

"A real princess would have a dragon to protect her!"

"Close your eyes," I said.

"Unlock the magic kingdom!

What do you see?"

"Nothing," said Alison.

"Listen!" I said.

"Do you hear the dragon

walking in the enchanted forest?"

"That's your dad walking down the hall,"

Rose said.

“Breathe!” I said.
“Do you smell the odor
of dragon breath in the air?”
“Oh, excuse me,” Molly said.
“I just burped!”

"Wait!" I said.

"Don't you hear the loud beating

of the dragon's heart?"

"That is my heart," said Rose.

"I've never seen a dragon before!"

“Now open your eyes,” I said.

“The dragon is here!

It is pink and it is breathing fire.

Look how spiky its tail is!”

"I see the dragon!" Alison said.

"It is sparkling in the moonlight."

The dragon smiled.

"She will protect us," I said.

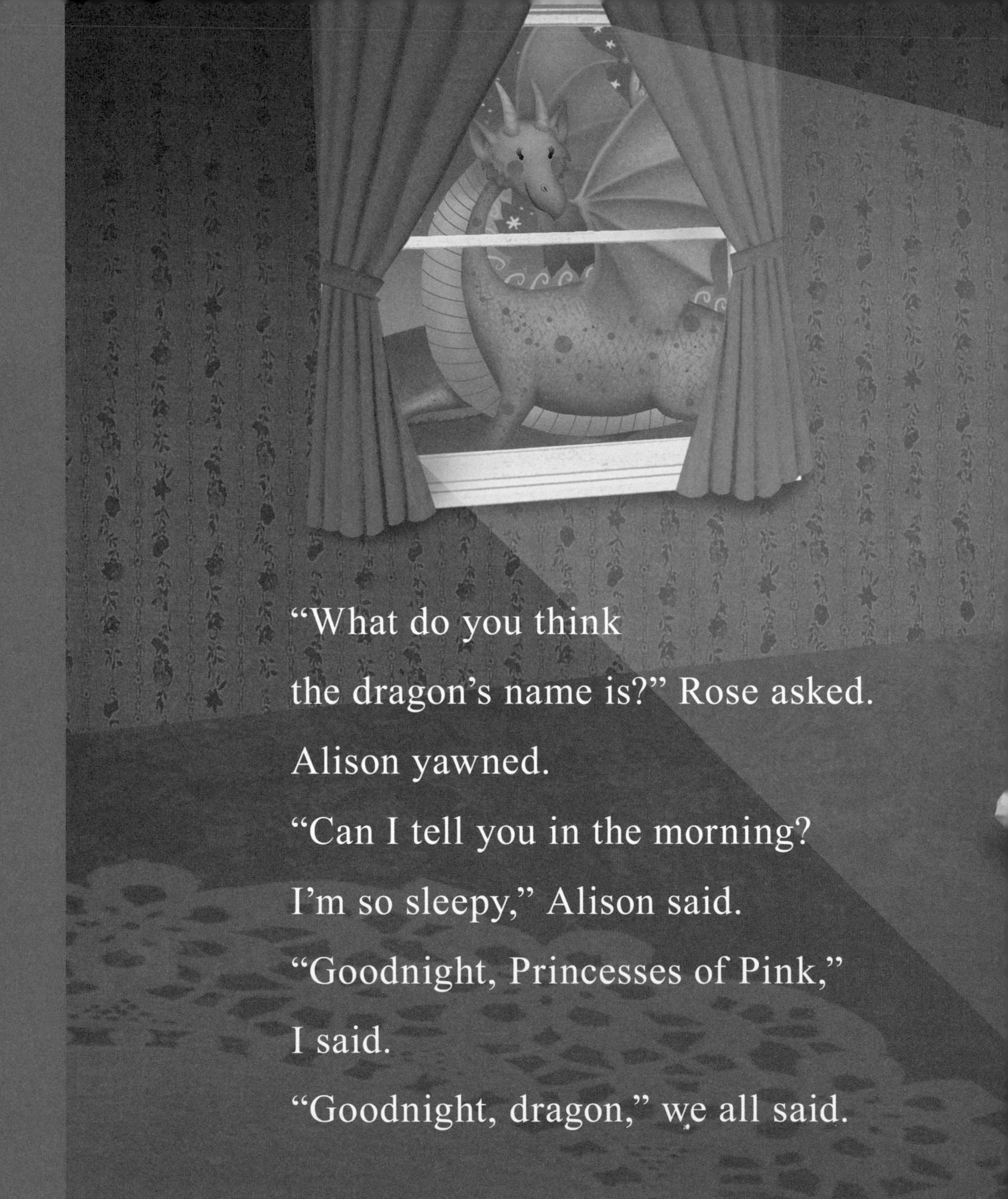

"What do you think
the dragon's name is?" Rose asked.
Alison yawned.
"Can I tell you in the morning?
I'm so sleepy," Alison said.
"Goodnight, Princesses of Pink,"
I said.
"Goodnight, dragon," we all said.

Outside, the dragon winked.

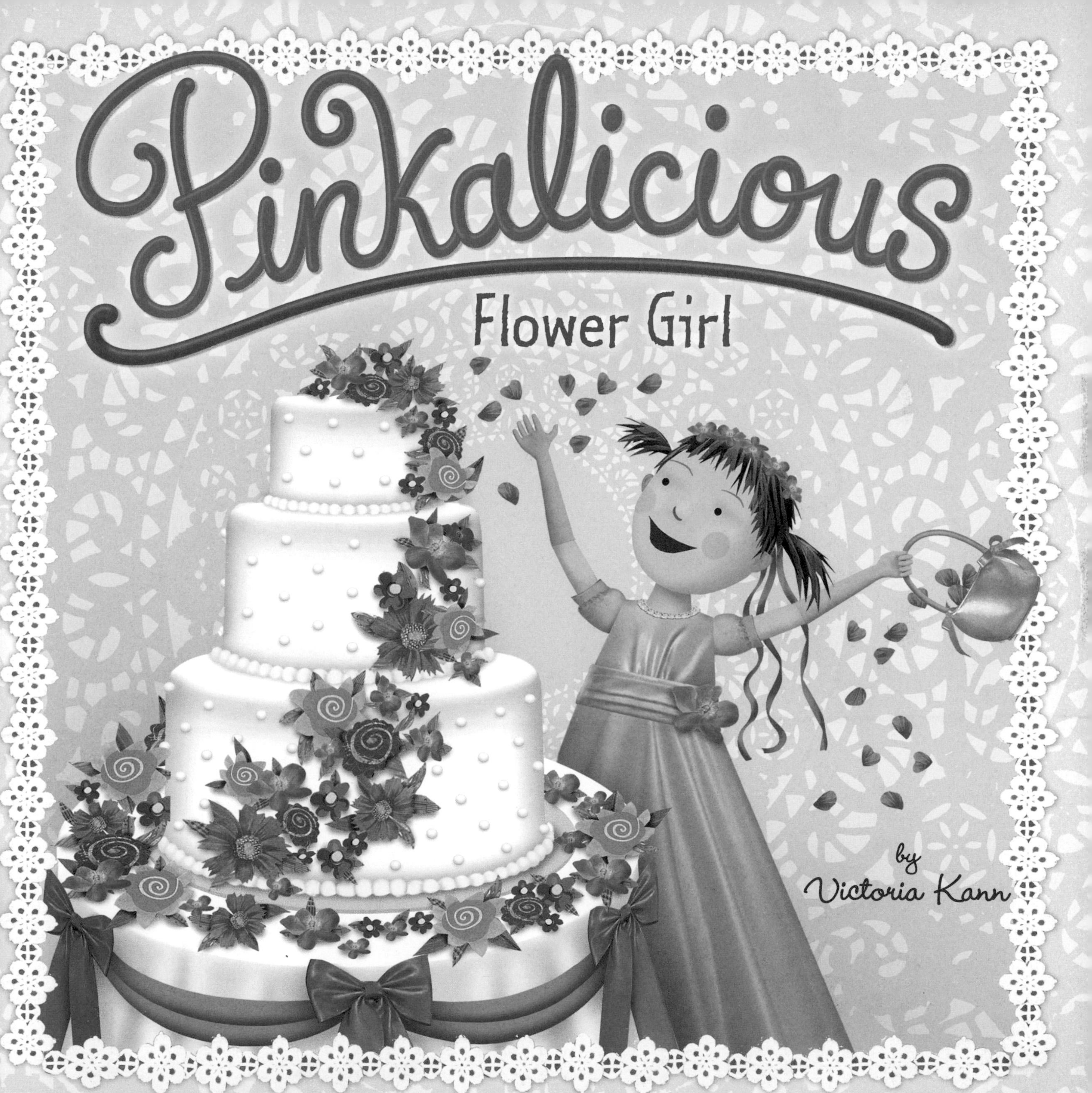
Pinkalicious
Flower Girl
by
Victoria Kann

For Libby!

xox,

Aunt Victoria

Pinkalicious®

Flower Girl

by Victoria Kann

Mommy was on the phone. I saw her smile and heard her say something about "a flower girl."

I wondered to myself, "What's a flower girl?"

cup
syrup
ter, and
ter is m
rop by sp
heavy p
cups suga
cup milk
stick marga

My mind filled with pinkatastic visions of flower girls. It was positively pinkerrific! I wanted to be a flower girl! I was going to start making my outfit right away!

I rounded up some useful supplies. My green tights were good for my stem. Then all I had to make were the perfect petals!

Peter asked, "What are you doing?"

I told him, "I'm a flower girl!"

"Wow," Peter said. "Can I be a flower boy? I want to be a tiger lily because it sounds ferocious!"

"I'm a fragrant rose," I said, squirting Mommy's perfume all over me.

As soon as our outfits were done, Peter and I rushed out into the sunshine.

Peter ran around yelling "Look out—I'm a flower! I'm a tiger lily!"

I twirled around. "Look how delicate my petals are! Don't I smell rosealicious?" I said.

News
Pinkville

"What are you doing? And what is that smell?" asked Daddy.

I was surprised that he couldn't tell just by looking at us. "Haven't you ever seen flower children before? I am a flower girl and Peter is a flower boy."

Daddy chuckled. "Mommy will tell you later, but flower girls don't smell or look like flowers—they *throw* flowers."

I was shocked. "Are you sure?"

Daddy laughed. "Yes, it's true. Flower girls really throw flowers."

Peter and I were stunned. I asked, "Why would flower girls throw flowers?"

Peter shrugged, then started picking flowers and tossing them all over the lawn.

I was completely confused. "People throw balls and sometimes horseshoes, or even tantrums. Why would anyone throw flowers? That just doesn't make sense!" I said.

News
Pinkville

Then it came to me! "Maybe Daddy meant *flour*, not flowers!" I shouted as I hurried into the kitchen.

"I don't get it," said Peter.
I shrugged and said, "Neither do I."

Throwing flour didn't make any more sense than throwing flowers, but it sure was fun! There was flour everywhere! It looked like there had been a blizzard inside the kitchen.

Peter laughed. "It's like having a snowball fight, but without the cold fingers!"

News
Pinkville

When Mommy walked into the kitchen, we both froze.

She stared at us. She stared at the room. It was a mess! Mommy was speechless. Finally she said, "Umm . . . what *are* you doing?"

When I told her, Mommy laughed so hard her face turned pink.

Then she explained what a flower girl is—and told me I was going to be one very soon! “My cousin wants you to be the flower girl at her wedding. Isn’t that great?”

Being a flower girl was even better than I had imagined. I was part of the wedding party, and I LOVE parties! I got to wear a pinkatastic dress, and I got to throw petals when the bride walked down the aisle. Peter got to be a ring bearer, which has NOTHING to do with bears. It means he got to carry the wedding rings. But the very best part . . .

. . . was the CAKE! Flower power forever!

Pinkalicious

Soccer Star

For Leigha,
my shining star!
—V.K.

by Victoria Kann

Daddy gave me a new pink soccer ball.
That pink ball inspired me
to kick and score like never before!

Pinksters

I couldn't wait
to play the first game of the year.
Our team is called the Pinksters.
They are the Ravens.

“Pink soccer balls are for babies,”
said Kendra.
Tiffany said, “Pink stinks.”

“Play ball!” said the coach.

“Think pink!” said Rose.

But I kept hearing Tiffany say
“Pink stinks.”
“I’ll show her pink does not stink,”
I said to Rose.

The ball came to me.

I kicked it.

It went too short.

Next the ball went too long.

Then it went crazy.

Oops!

I kicked the ball to Tiffany

by mistake.

She scored a goal.
The score was one for them,
zero for the Pinksters.

Rose scored a goal.

"Good job, Rose!" I said.

The score was tied.

One for them, one for us,

and two minutes left to play.

Then Kendra kicked the ball.

The ball sailed up high.

I heard *Pink stinks*

inside my head.

I had to get that ball!

As I ran to the ball,

Goldilicious galloped toward me.

She scooped me up on her back.

We left the park far below.

We flew across the sky.

We saw girls playing soccer
all over the world!

We flew to the pink sands of Egypt.

I made a great pass!

I did a corner kick to Spain.

"¡Pensar en rosa!" a girl said to me.

That's "Think pink!" in Spanish.

Cherry blossoms bloomed in China.
The girls cheered "Think pink!"
in Chinese.
"*Shi fěnhóng!*"

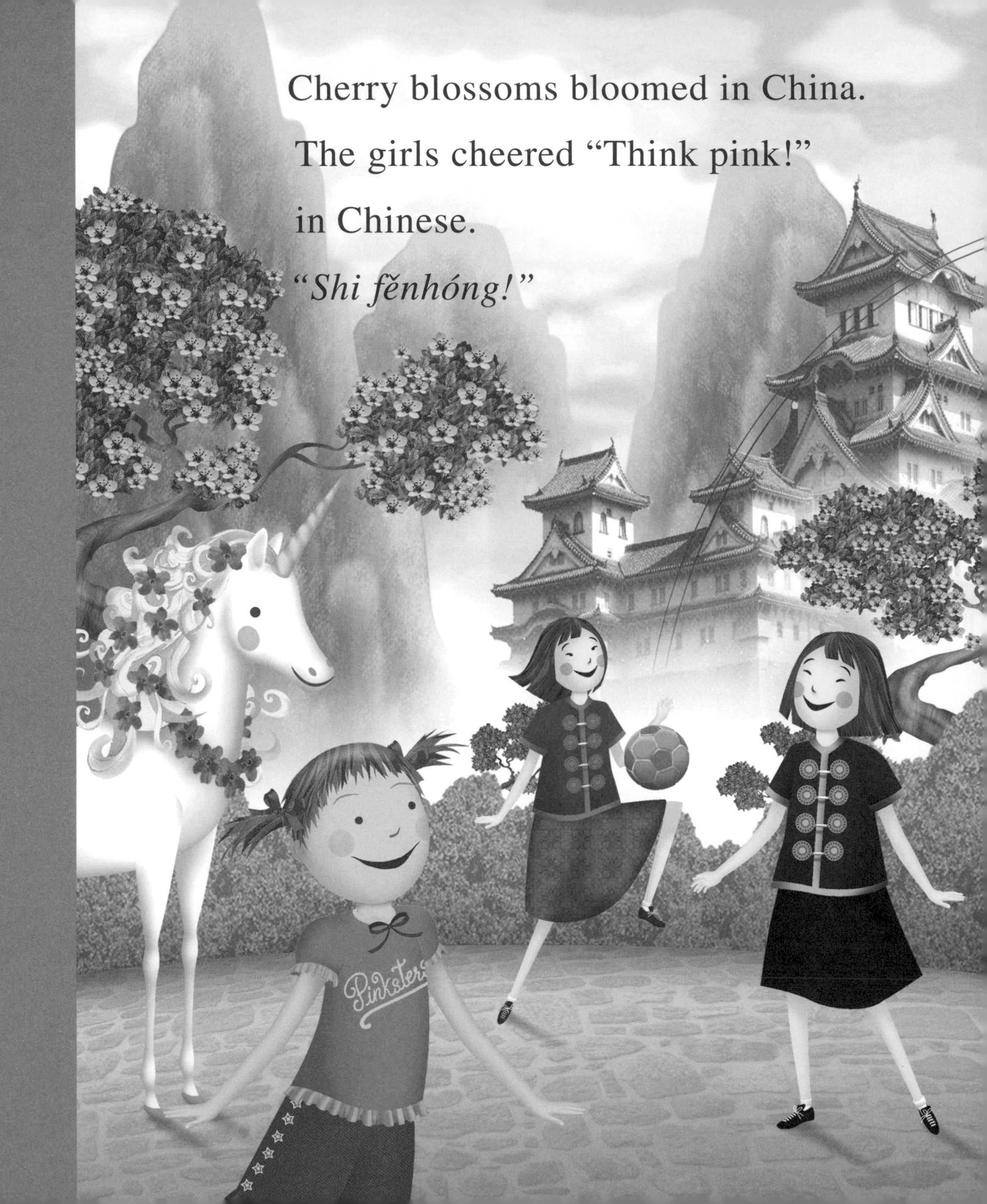

By the time we got to Italy,

I forgot all about mean old Tiffany.

"Goldilicious, let's get back
to the game," I said.
"I've learned so much.
I think I know what to do now."

I ran.

I got the ball.

I took aim and I kicked.

I did it!

I scored!

The Pinksters won.

“Wow, good job!” said Kendra.

“Pink?” said Tiffany.

“It doesn’t stink.”

"Three cheers for Pinkalicious!"
said Rose.
I cheered, too.

Three cheers for
pink soccer players
everywhere!

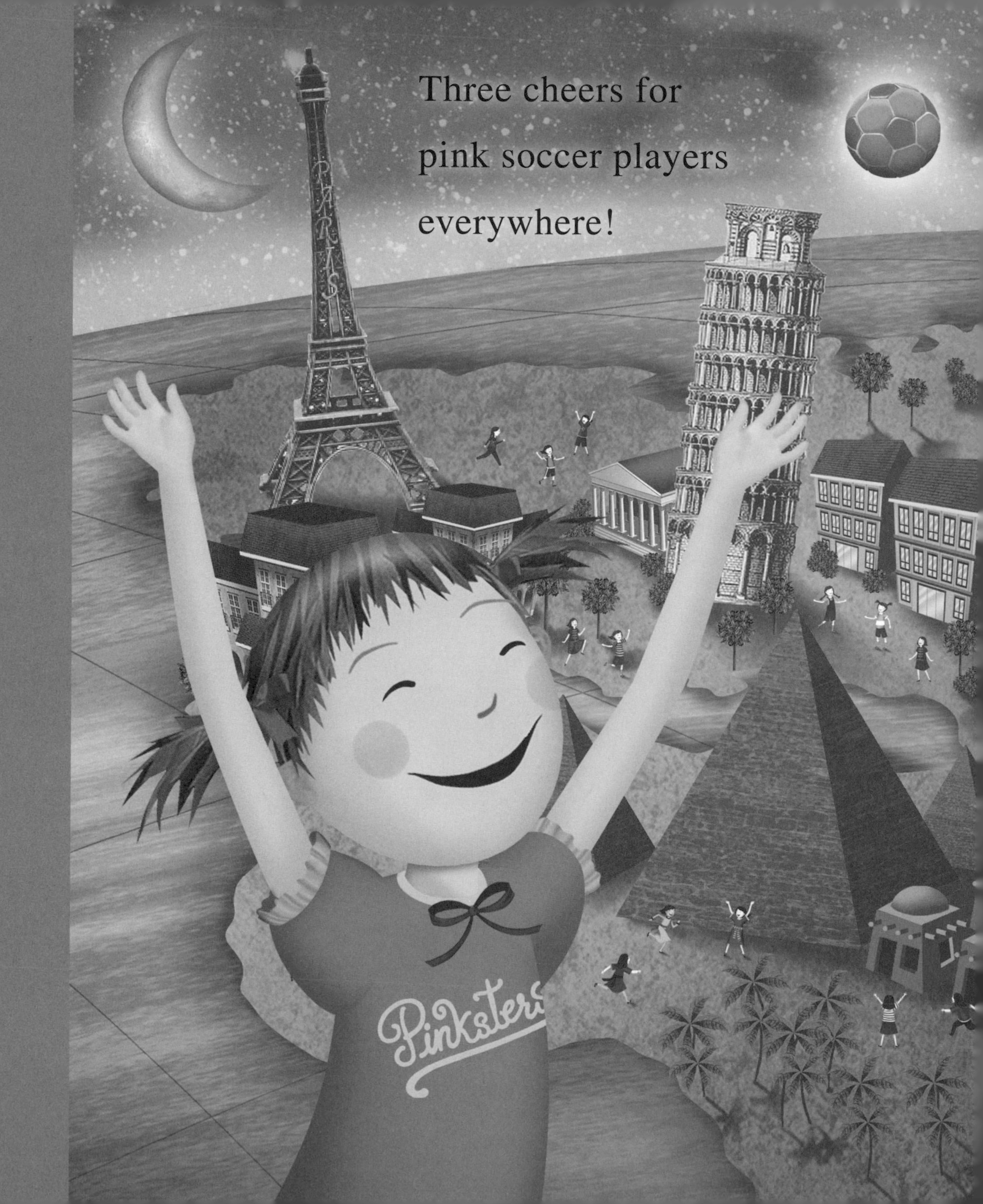

Pinkalicious
and the Pinkatastic
Zoo Day
by
Victoria Kann

For Megan!

xox,

Aunt Victoria

by Victoria Kann

One sunny Saturday,

I squeezed my teddy bear tight.

"Guess what, Henrietta," I said.

"It's Teddy Bear Day at the zoo!"

"I'm bringing Fred," said Peter.

At the zoo, we walked by the zebras.

"These guys could use

a hint of pink," I said to myself.

I waved my wand and pink-a-presto!
A zebra changed the color of
its stripes.

“Pink!” I waved my wand at the lions.

The hippos and rhinos came next.

“Pink! Pink!” I commanded.

"What are you doing, Pinkalicious?"

asked Peter.

I waved my wand at him, too.

Then I remembered the teddy bear picnic.

I love teddy bears and picnics!

Peter and I gave Fred and Henrietta
teddy-back rides down the path.
The Teddy Bear Day fun was starting!
We got bear-shaped balloons.

We spread out a large blanket.
We sipped honey tea
and ate teddy bear cookies.
Peter gave Fred a sip of tea, too.
"Fred says this tea is BEARY good,"
said Peter.

I couldn't wait to see
the real bears,
but when we got to the bears
they were all sleeping.
It was boring to watch.

“Pinkalicious!” Peter pointed.
I looked up and gasped.
Above us, a vine led from
the monkey house to a field.
One monkey was crossing over!

The little monkey
did tricks on the vine.
She swung from side to side.
She hung upside down by her tail.

I didn't want Henrietta to miss out,
so Daddy put her on his shoulder.

I saw the monkey look at Henrietta.

She clapped her hands and hooted.

I had a funny feeling that something bad was about to happen.

“Oh, no!” I cried
as the monkey swung down low.
She scooped up Henrietta!
“Well I’ll be a monkey’s uncle,”
Daddy said, amazed.

I watched as the monkey scurried over to the field. "She thinks Henrietta is her teddy bear," Peter said.

The monkey rocked Henrietta
and gave her a big hug.
Peter laughed.
But I didn't think it was funny.
Not one little bit.

I tried everything to get the monkey
to bring Henrietta back.
I sang to her.
I made silly faces at her.
I even asked Peter to try
speaking in monkey to her.
Nothing worked!
She kept on playing with Henrietta.
"You're making a monkey
out of my teddy bear!" I said.

“I’m sorry, Pinkalicious,”
said Mommy.
“The zoo is closing.
We have to go.”

"Oh, no! This is unbearable.

What about Henrietta?" I said.

I started to cry.

"We'll think of something,"

Daddy promised.

I didn't know what else to do.

At home, all I could think about
was poor Henrietta.
I loved her so much.
How could I explain that
to a monkey?

Suddenly, I had an idea.

"Quick, Peter," I said.

I told him my plan.

We got right to work.

The next day,

we got to the zoo bright and early.

I found the little monkey right away.

“I have a gift for you,” I said.
I held up the snuggly sock monkey
that Peter and I had made.

"Now watch me," I told the monkey.

I gave the new toy a squeeze.

The monkey hugged Henrietta.

I patted the sock monkey's head.

The little monkey patted Henrietta.

I tossed the sock monkey into the field.

The monkey tossed Henrietta over to me!

I picked up my teddy bear

and the little monkey

picked up her new friend.

"Good-bye!" I waved.

"It was fun monkeying around with you!"

The author gratefully acknowledges the artistic and editorial contributions of Robert Masheris, Natalie Engel, Jared Osterhold, Daniel Griffo, Wendy Wax, Susan Hill, and Justine Fontes.

Based on the HarperCollins book *Pinkalicious* written by Victoria Kann and Elizabeth Kann, illustrated by Victoria Kann

For information address HarperCollins Children's Books, a division of HarperCollins Publishers,
195 Broadway, New York, NY 10007.
www.harpercollinschildrens.com

ISBN 978-0-06-218800-7
Book design by Theresa Venezia

14 15 SCP 10 9 8

First Edition

Have you read all of these *Pinkalicious*® books?

- ☐ Pinkalicious
- ☐ Purplicious
- ☐ Goldilicious
- ☐ Silverlicious
- ☐ Emeraldalicious
- ☐ Love, Pinkalicious Reusable Sticker Book
- ☐ Pinkalicious and the Pink Drink
- ☐ Pinkalicious: School Rules!
- ☐ Pinkalicious: Tickled Pink
- ☐ Pinkalicious: Pink around the Rink
- ☐ Pinkalicious: The Perfectly Pink Collection
- ☐ Pinkalicious: Pinkadoodles
- ☐ Pinkalicious: Pinkie Promise
- ☐ Pinkalicious and the Pink Pumpkin
- ☐ Pinkalicious: The Pinkerrific Playdate
- ☐ Pinkalicious: The Princess of Pink Treasury
- ☐ Pinkalicious: Pink of Hearts
- ☐ Pinkalicious: The Pinkatastic Giant Sticker Book
- ☐ Pinkalicious and the Pink Hat Parade
- ☐ Pinkalicious: The Princess of Pink Slumber Party
- ☐ Pinkalicious: Pink-a-rama
- ☐ Pinkalicious: Soccer Star
- ☐ Pinkalicious: Purpledoodles
- ☐ Pinkalicious: Pink, Pink, Hooray!
- ☐ Pinkalicious and the Pinkatastic Zoo Day
- ☐ Pinkalicious: Teeny Tiny Pinky Library
- ☐ Pinkalicious: Fairy House
- ☐ Pinkalicious: Pinkafy Your World
- ☐ Pinkalicious: Flower Girl
- ☐ Pinkalicious: Goldidoodles
- ☐ Pinkalicious: Puptastic

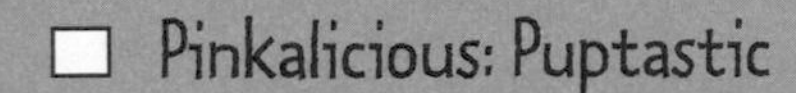